MY ADVENTURES
IN
Disney · PI
TOY STORY 2

D0000106

This book was especially written for
Derek Rasmussen
With love from
Nana and Papa

Adapted by Wendy Elks
ISBN 1 875676 13 9

It was October 31st, Derek's birthday, and he had invited Alex, Gabe and Sarah over for a birthday celebration. He had spent all morning decorating his room with colorful balloons and there was a big red banner on the wall which read 'HAPPY BIRTHDAY, DEREK!'

While he waited for his friends to arrive, Derek sat down to watch his favorite video, *Toy Story 2*. After a while he felt himself becoming sleepy. His eyes closed gently and he drifted off to sleep. All of a sudden, in his dream, he was in the same room that had been on his TV screen moments before and he was the same size as the toys. He had become one of them!

Buzz the space ranger and Rex the dinosaur were playing a video game. Then Buzz saw Derek. 'Hey, a new toy! What's your name?'

'I'm Derek,' said Derek.

'Do you live here now?' asked Buzz.

'No, I live at 8415 230 Way Northeast in Redmond. Somehow I've become a toy like you.'

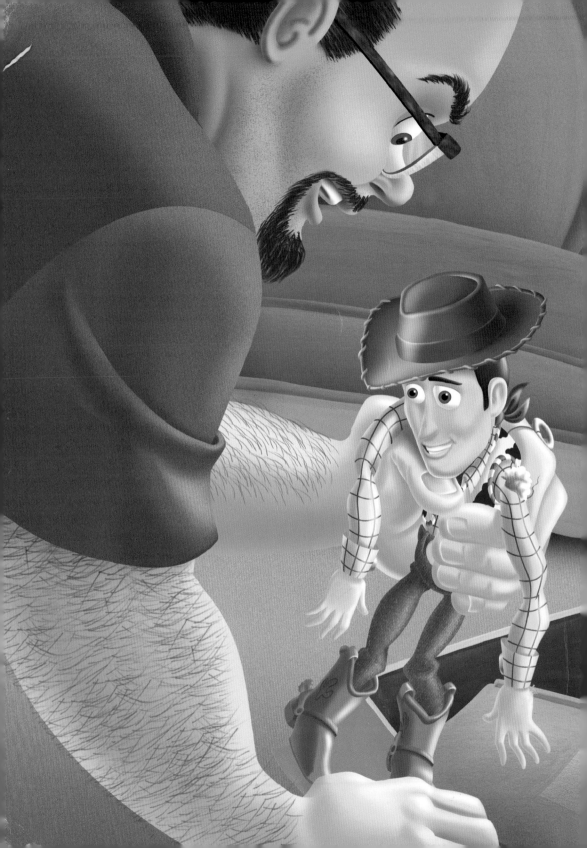

'That's great, you can be our friend and come and live with us in Andy's room. Andy is our owner,' said Rex. 'Do you want to have a turn at playing our video game?'

'Yes, please!' said Derek.

Rex seemed to be looking around for something. 'Hey, where's Woody?' he said. Everyone looked for Woody, but he couldn't be found anywhere.

'He's lost!' said Buzz. 'Andy is going to be so upset!'

Derek climbed up onto Andy's desk to look out the window. It was difficult because he was so small now. 'Maybe he's outside,' he suggested. The other toys clambered up, too.

Earlier, Andy's Mom had taken Wheezy to sell at a garage sale. Woody rode Andy's dog, Buster, into the yard and grabbed onto Wheezy. But before they could get back inside, Woody fell off.

'There's Woody!' cried Buzz. Woody was lying near some boxes. Just then a man came along. He picked Woody up and ran off towards his car.

'Hey! Woody's being kidnapped!' cried Mr. Potato Head.

The license plate on the car reads **LZTYBRN**.

In a flash, Buzz jumped out of the window and slid down the drainpipe. He raced towards the car, but it was too late; the car had sped away. A chicken feather flew out of the window and floated to the ground near Buzz. He picked it up, and slowly went back to the others.

'We got the license plate number of the car!' said Derek. 'We're going to try to find out who it belongs to!'

Buzz held up the feather. 'This might be a clue,' he said.

Derek punched in the letters from the number plate on Mr. Spell.

'Hmm, L-Z-T-Y-B-R-N. What could that mean?' wondered Derek.

'I know!' shouted Buzz. 'It stands for Al's Toy Barn! This chicken feather is part of the outfit that Al wears in his commercials!'

'I know where Al's Toy Barn is!' said Derek.

'Great, Derek!' said Slinky.

Derek turned to Etch and asked him to make a map.

'But how do we get there?' asked Mr. Potato Head.

Buzz stood up tall in front of everyone and, with a pencil as a pointer, he showed the others where they needed to go to save their friend. 'We'll walk if we have to!' he said. 'We have to save Woody! Let's go!'

The toys crept out onto the roof of the house. Bo Peep and the others watched as Slinky helped Derek, Rex, Mr. Potato Head, Hamm and Buzz jump down to the yard below. It made Derek's tummy tickle to fly through the air like that. Then off they all went, creeping through the streets toward Al's Toy Barn.

Meanwhile, in the back room at Al's Toy Barn, Al was getting into his chicken suit to do another commercial. He had put Woody into a special display case. Al was excited because Woody was worth a lot of money as a collector's item.

'This Woody doll makes my *Woody's Roundup* set complete! I'll make a fortune!' sang Al. Then he left the room, locking the door behind him.

As soon as Al was gone, Woody came to life. He wriggled out of the display case and looked around. How was he going to escape and get back home? He discovered an air vent, but before he could escape through it, the toys appeared. One was a cowgirl, and the other was a jolly-looking horse. A wise-looking old Prospector doll waved and smiled at Woody.

'It's you! It's you!' the cowgirl cried happily. The horse neighed with excitement.

'Who are you?' asked Woody in surprise.

'I'm Jessie, and this here is Bullseye! He's your horse!' cried Jessie.

Bullseye licked Woody happily on the face.

'I don't have a horse!' said Woody, wiping his face. 'And how do you know who I am?'

'You don't know who you are, do you?' said Jessie in amazement. 'Why, you're a famous TV star, Woody. You had your own program and everything! Look at this.' Jessie switched on the TV. Woody couldn't believe it. He saw himself riding Bullseye and singing a song.

'Wow,' he said after a while. 'That's great, but all I really want to do is go back home to my owner, Andy, and all of my friends.'

'You can't,' said Jessie. 'Now that Al has you, we're all going to be sold to a museum in Japan.'

Woody was horrified. 'Oh, no!' he cried. 'That's terrible! I'll never see Andy again!'

'Oh, well,' said Jessie. 'At least you have us! We're a complete set!'

Woody was unhappy, but he then thought about it a little. It might be fun to live in the Japanese museum like a star!

Meanwhile, Derek and the toys had finally reached Al's Toy Barn. Now there was just a very busy road to cross!

'I'll be turned into mash on that road!' cried Mr. Potato Head.

Buzz noticed a pile of traffic cones. 'Maybe we can use these,' he said.

'Yes!' cried Derek. 'We can hide underneath them! The cars will go around them, and we'll be able to get across.'

'Great idea, Derek!' Buzz agreed.

Derek and Buzz put cones over the others and then themselves. They waited until there was a gap in the traffic, and then they started to cross the road. There was a sound of screeching tires.

'Go! Go, everyone! Don't stop now!' cried Buzz. Somehow they all made it safely across.

Before long the toys and Derek were inside the store.

'Where do we go now?' asked Slinky, gazing at the long rows of shelves stacked high with toys.

'Split up,' said Buzz in his best commando's voice. 'We'll each do an aisle and meet at the back of the store. Make sure nobody sees you!'

Derek felt like a little mouse, creeping along behind boxes and dolls and soft toys. Soon they were all gathered together at the back of the store. No one had seen any sign of poor Woody. Then Derek heard a voice coming from an open door.

'That's Al,' he whispered to the others. They crept to the door and listened.

Al was on the phone. 'Yes, I have the Woody doll,' he was saying. 'I can bring the whole set tonight. My flight leaves at seven.'

The toys and Derek looked at each other in horror. Woody was being taken far away — on a plane. Tonight! He'd be lost forever unless they did something!

'We've got to go, too,' whispered Buzz. 'It's our only chance to save Woody.' Derek and the toys crept into the open briefcase next to Al's desk.

Al hung up the phone. 'I gotta finish packing,' he muttered to himself, as he hurried from the room and went across the street to his apartment.

Back at Al's apartment, Derek and the toys crept out of the briefcase and prepared to take Woody home — but he didn't want to go! Now that he knew he was a valuable toy, he wanted to go with the Roundup gang and live in the Japanese museum.

'Woody,' said Buzz, 'you are a toy. You have to come home and be there for Andy when *he* needs you!' But Woody wouldn't listen. Slowly Buzz turned and walked away. Then he heard something.

'Buzz! Wait! I'm coming with you,' cried Woody. He realized that Buzz was right — a child's love was more important.

But it was too late! Al came in and packed Woody and the Roundup gang into a green case. The toys had to move fast if they were going to save Woody! They made it to the airport just in time and hid inside a pet carrier which started moving along a conveyor belt along with hundreds of other bags going in all directions. Luckily, they caught up with the green case containing Woody and the Roundup toys. Buzz lifted the lid and managed to free Woody.

Woody waved wildly to Buzz to let him know that they still had work to do!

'Jessie and Bullseye want to come, too!' he shouted to Buzz. Bullseye climbed out, but before Jessie could follow, the box had fallen through a hole!

'You follow Jessie!' Derek called to Buzz. 'I'll look after the others!'

Buzz saluted Derek. Then he, Woody and Bullseye disappeared through the hole. As the others were about to fall through the hole too, Derek grabbed them and jumped off the belt.

Once they were safe, they peered through the hole. There had been a baggage train underneath it but it was driving away, and Buzz and Woody, riding Bullseye, were chasing after it!

Derek watched as Bullseye, Buzz and Woody chased after the plane.

Bravely, Jessie leapt down from the plane's baggage compartment onto Bullseye.

'Hooray!' cheered the toys. 'What a team! Buzz, Woody and Derek have saved the day!'

'Now, how do we get home?' wondered Mr. Potato Head.

Derek looked around and saw an empty baggage train standing nearby.

'Well, we've done well together so far,' he said. 'Do you think that, between us, we can drive home in that baggage train?'

So that was exactly what they did. They climbed back up the drainpipe into Andy's room, and they cheered each other and did high-fives to celebrate their success.

'Thanks for helping us so much, Derek!' said Woody. Bullseye licked Derek's cheek.

Then they heard the bedroom door open. Derek started to feel funny again. The toys seemed to be getting smaller and smaller. Then he realized that it was he who was getting bigger! All at once he was normal-sized, and sitting on the chair in his room. The *Toy Story 2* video was still playing.

Alex, Gabe and Sarah were walking into the room carrying a large cake with candles on it. 'Oh, there you are, Derek,' said Alex. We've been looking for you to blow out the candles on your birthday cake.'

Derek smiled and replied 'Oh, I was having such fun playing with Woody and the other toys.'

This personalized Disney/Pixar Toy Story 2 book was specially created for Derek Rasmussen of 8415 230 Way Northeast, Redmond WA with love from Nana and Papa.

Additional books ordered may be mailed separately - please allow a few days for differences in delivery times.

If you would like to receive additional My Adventure Book order forms, please contact:

My Adventure Books
PO Box 9203
Central Islip NY 11722-9203

Phone: (717) 918 1068
www.identitydirect.com